Dark Man

Dying for
the Dark

by Peter Lancett

illustrated by Jan Pedroietta

Rans✿m

Chapter One:
In the Rain

In the bad part of the city, there is a warehouse.

It has not been used for many years, and the roof has fallen in.

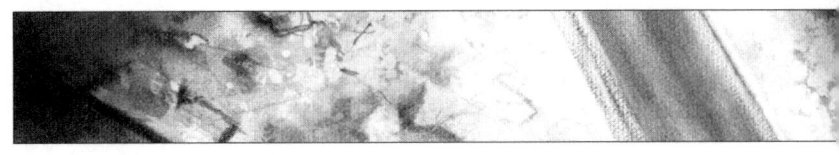

The floor of the warehouse is made of concrete.

It is covered with broken roof tiles and rubbish.

There is a lot of broken glass.

It is night and it is cold. Heavy rain lashes down.

A girl is lying on her back.

She does not move, but she is breathing.

She is a friend of the Dark Man and had come with a message for him.

The Dark Man kneels beside her.

They are both soaked from the rain.

The Dark Man strokes the girl's hair.

Her eyes do not open, but she smiles.

The Dark Man takes off his coat. He does not care about the cold or the rain. He only cares about the girl.

Her T-shirt is ripped where she was injured.

The Dark Man had arrived too late to protect her from a man with a knife.

Now he just hopes that he can save her. She has lost a lot of blood.

He puts his coat over her and lifts her into his arms.

The Dark Man must get the girl to a hospital.

The nearest hospital is on the far side of the
city, and he must carry her there.

The girl moans as he begins to walk, but she
does not open her eyes.

Chapter Two:
Three Figures

As he steps over the rubble, the Dark Man feels that he is being watched.

He thinks he hears voices behind him, but when he turns there is no one there.

Only flickering, dark shadows.

With the girl in his arms, he keeps on walking.

Soon he is on the streets. There are no people on the streets, because of the cold and the rain.

The night-time is never safe in the bad part of the city.

Only a few street lights are working, as the Dark Man carries the girl.

Most of the buildings are empty and ruined, but in some there are lights on.

These are the poor people who cannot leave the bad part of the city.

The Dark Man knows that most of them are good people.

It seems that no one cares about these people, but the Dark Man cares.

The Dark Man lives here with them. He helps them when he can.

Now he must help the girl.

Far ahead, the Dark Man sees three figures standing in the glow of a street light.

The Dark Man is not afraid, but he does not imagine that these are good people.

They seem to be waiting for him to get near.

Soon, the Dark Man can see that they look like men.

He wonders if they might be demons, sent by the Shadow Masters.

The Shadow Masters can use magic to make demons look like men.

Chapter Three:
"Who Are Your Masters?"

The Dark Man stops before he reaches the men, but says nothing.

"Where are you taking her?" one of the men asks.

"I am taking her to the hospital across the city," the Dark Man says.

"What is wrong with her?" another man asks.

The Dark Man can see that this man is holding a knife. The knife blade flashes under the street light.

"She has lost a lot of blood," the Dark Man says. "I must hurry."

The third man steps into the light, shaking his head.

In his hand he is holding a baseball bat.

"We cannot allow you to take her anywhere," this third man says. "You must leave her with us."

The three men move slowly towards the Dark Man.

The Dark Man notices that the knife blade is stained with blood.

The man holding the knife grins and nods.

"Yes, you startled us earlier," he says. "Or we would have finished the job there and then."

The Dark Man gently places the girl on the ground and stands between her and the men.

"Getting rid of both of you is going to please our masters," the man with the baseball bat says.

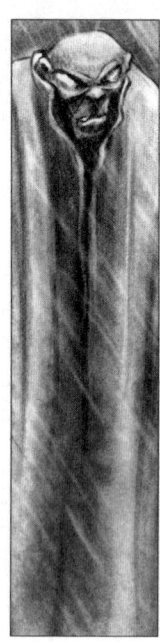

"Just who are your masters?" the Dark Man asks.

"I think you know," the man with the knife says, looking up to the roof of a building across the road.

The Dark Man gazes up through the lashing rain and sees a hooded figure looking down.

It is a Shadow Master!

The Dark Man kicks the baseball bat out of the hand that holds it.

It skids into the gutter, as the Dark Man pushes the man backwards.

The man stumbles into his partner and falls back onto the knife blade.

The blade plunges into his back.

There is a scream that is louder than the howling wind.

Orange light bursts out from the wounded man's mouth. The skin seems to melt from his face.

The man was a demon after all - a fire demon!

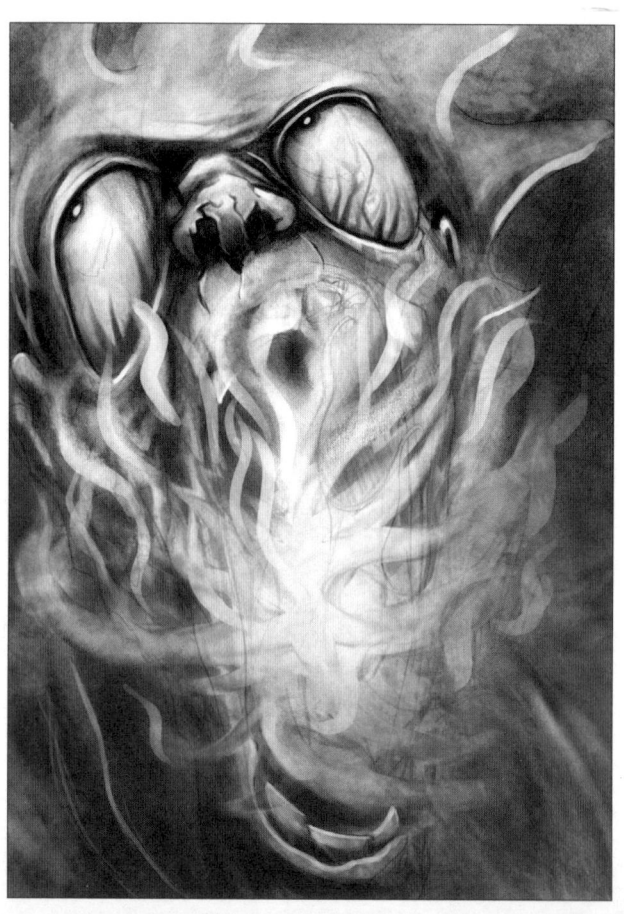

Chapter Four:
Evil Magic

The Dark Man watches as the driving rain melts the fire demon.

The two other demons stand back.

The Dark Man can see fear in their faces.

They are afraid that, if they are injured, they will also be destroyed by the rain.

The Shadow Masters have given them skin, but it can easily be removed.

The Dark Man reaches down and picks up the baseball bat.

He swings it at the two demons.

The demons scream and leap back. Then they turn and run.

From the rooftop, the Shadow Master screams.

The Dark Man wants to chase the demons and destroy them, but he cannot. The girl needs him.

He picks her up, but now she does not smile.

The Dark Man walks as quickly as he can.

He must get her to the hospital.

The evil magic of the Shadow Masters is still in the air.

This evil magic feeds on suffering and death.